Liam's Extraordinary Adventure

Welcome to "Liam's Extraordinary Adventure"! Kids will love this special book with colourful illustrations and simple language. Join Liam on an exciting journey through **Northern Ireland**, where you can imagine yourself as the main character. Explore beautiful landscapes, learn about geography, and let your imagination soar! Get ready for an extraordinary adventure!

Second Edition, 2024

Chapter 1: The Mysterious Visitor

Liam loved exploring new places in Northern Ireland. One day, a beautiful bird named Celestia came to his house. Celestia had shiny, colourful feathers that looked like they were made of stardust. She was very special because she could change into different kinds of birds, turning their ordinary day into an extraordinary adventure!

Chapter 2: Puzzle of the Giants

Together, Liam and Celestia, in her magnificent form, set off on a journey. Their first stop was the **Giant's Causeway**, a place filled with rocks that looked like pieces of a giant's puzzle. Liam marvelled at the legend of Finn McCool and walked upon the rocks, feeling the magic beneath his feet.

Chapter 3: The Mountain's Fairy Tale

For their next adventure, Celestia transformed into a soaring eagle, and Liam climbed upon her back. They ventured to the **Mourne Mountains**, where Liam felt like he had stepped into a fairy tale. As they reached the summit of the tallest mountain, Liam gazed at the panoramic view, imagining himself as a hero in a storybook.

Chapter 4: Secrets of the Antrim Coast

Taking the form of a graceful seagull, Celestia and Liam continued their journey to the enchanting **Antrim Coast**. Liam witnessed towering cliffs and crashing waves, while Celestia gracefully glided through the air. They explored the rocky shores together, discovering a hidden world of curious sea creatures, each one more astonishing than the last.

Chapter 5: The Frozen Remnants

For their final adventure, Celestia transformed into a beautiful swan. Liam and Celestia embarked on a boat, gliding across the calm waters of **Lough Neagh**. As they floated, Liam learned that the lake was once a vast expanse of ice blocks, now melted away but leaving behind a breath-taking legacy.

Chapter 6: Farewell for Now

As their journey came to an end, Liam's heart swelled with gratitude for the magical experiences he had shared with Celestia. With a promise to return one day, Liam bid farewell to his extraordinary friend, knowing that the spirit of adventure would forever remain in his heart.

Chapter 7: The Wonders of Queen's University Belfast

Liam loved learning and wanted to know more about Northern Ireland. He found a book about **Queen's University Belfast**, a special place where people went to learn and grow. Liam imagined himself exploring the beautiful buildings and gardens, full of excitement and curiosity.

Chapter 8: The Enchanted Library

Liam followed enchanted footprints to a secret library in the university. Its books and maps held ancient stories and secrets. Liam's fingers tingled as he picked up a book called "The Magical History of Northern Ireland". Its pages came alive with colourful pictures and exciting tales of heroes and legends.

Chapter 9: The Quest for Knowledge

Inspired by these stories, Liam embarked on a quest for knowledge. He visited different parts of Queen's University Belfast. In the Science Building, Liam learned about the wonders of the universe and carried out fun experiments. At the Art School, he discovered his love for painting and sculpture. Liam created beautiful art that showcased the beauty of Northern Ireland.

Chapter 10: Unravelling Mysteries at Ulster University

Liam was hungry to learn more, so he visited **Ulster University**. He explored the Magee campus and met clever professors and students who were doing exciting research. They taught him about archaeology and technology, and he even tried coding to create his own virtual worlds. Ulster University was full of incredible discoveries!

Chapter 11: The Magical Geography Lesson

Liam felt like a teacher and transformed his room into an imaginary magical classroom. He showed his pupils maps and told them stories about the amazing places he had visited. They felt inspired to explore the world and learn new things just like Liam.

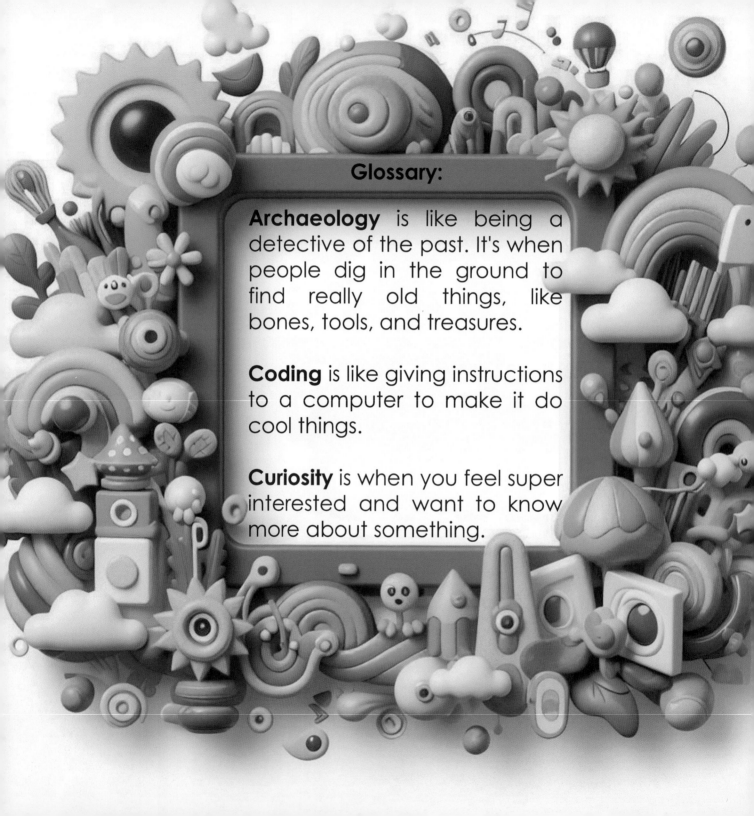

Glossary:

Archaeology is like being a detective of the past. It's when people dig in the ground to find really old things, like bones, tools, and treasures.

Coding is like giving instructions to a computer to make it do cool things.

Curiosity is when you feel super interested and want to know more about something.

Glossary:

Enchanted is when something feels like magic or is very, very special and wonderful.

Farewell means saying goodbye to friends or people you care about. It's like wishing them well and hoping to see them again soon.

Glossary:

Gratitude is a fancy word for saying 'thank you' and feeling really happy about something nice someone did for you.

Legacy is like leaving behind something really important or special for others to remember.

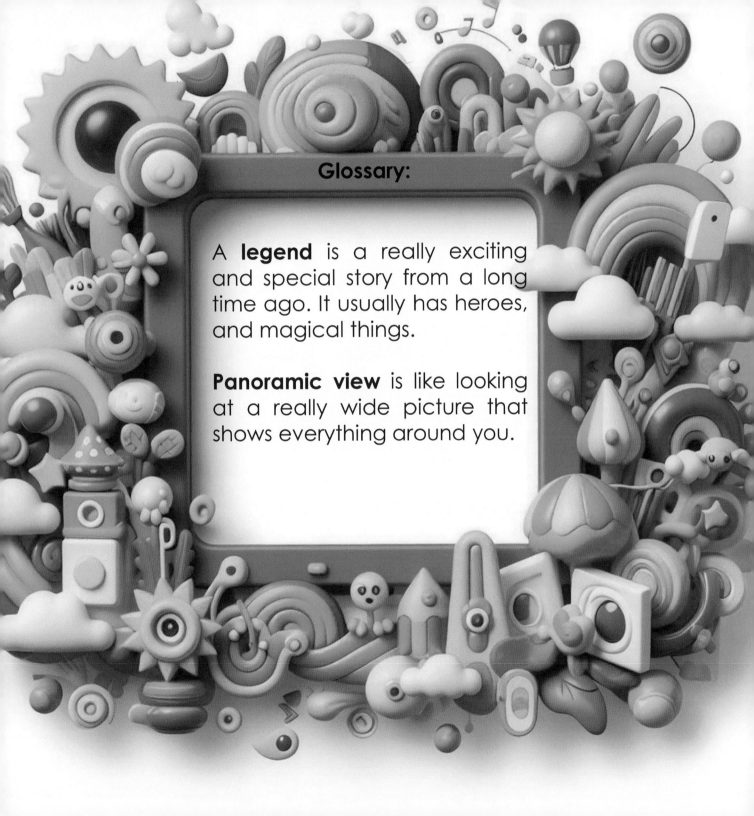

Glossary:

A **legend** is a really exciting and special story from a long time ago. It usually has heroes, and magical things.

Panoramic view is like looking at a really wide picture that shows everything around you.

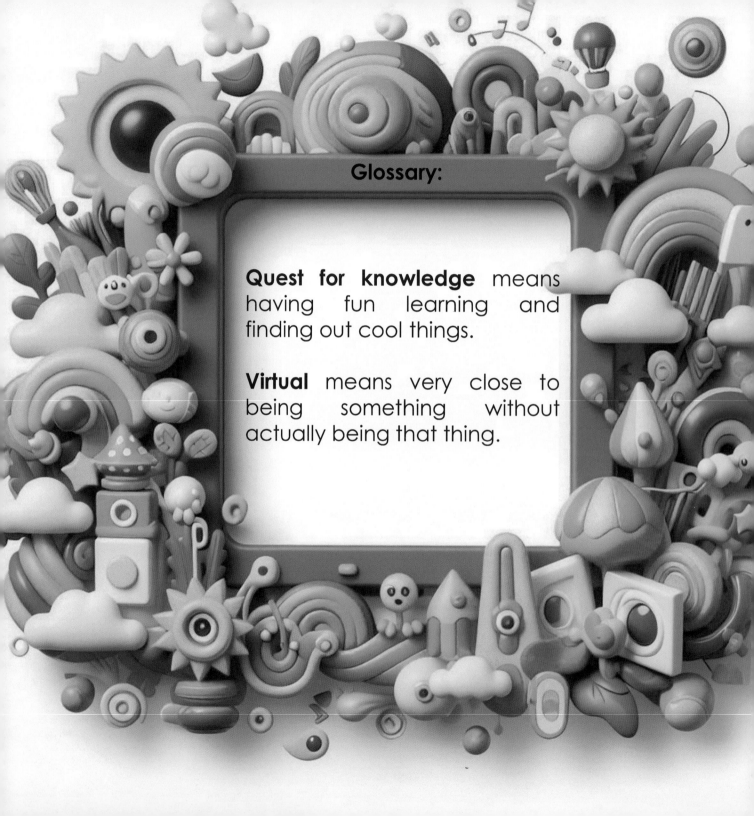

Glossary:

Quest for knowledge means having fun learning and finding out cool things.

Virtual means very close to being something without actually being that thing.

About the Author

"**Orbiting Oceans**" is a pseudonym for a highly accomplished scientist who holds a PhD, MSc, and BSc in Geographic Information Science. Orbiting Oceans has become a specialist in the use of geographic information systems (GIS) via years of expertise in the field and has contributed to numerous research publications. Orbiting Oceans is now transferring their knowledge to the field of children's literature with a series of books designed to excite and educate young readers.

SCAN ME

About the Books

Welcome to the enchanting world of "**Orbital Adventures**"! Immerse yourself in thrilling journeys to far-flung destinations, where vibrant illustrations and accessible language captivate young readers. Let their imaginations soar as they embark on extraordinary quests. Explore other books in our captivating series and follow us on Facebook for updates. Find our books on **Amazon** and delight in limitless possibilities!

SCAN ME

Printed in Great Britain
by Amazon